SUPER DC HEROES

BATMAN

POISON IVY'S DEADLY GARDEN

WRITTEN BY
BLAKE A. HOENA

ILLUSTRATED BY
ERIK DOESCHER,
MIKE DeCARLO, AND
LEE LOUGHRIDGE

BATMAN CREATED BY
BOB KANE

STONE ARCH BOOKS
MINNEAPOLIS   SAN DIEGO

Published by Stone Arch Books in 2009
151 Good Counsel Drive, P.O. Box 669
Mankato, Minnesota 56002
www.stonearchbooks.com

Library of Congress Cataloging-in-Publication Data
Hoena, B. A.
    Poison Ivy's Deadly Garden / by Blake A. Hoena; illustrated by Erik
Doescher.
        p. cm. — (DC Super Heroes. Batman)
        ISBN 978-1-4342-1152-1 (library binding)
        ISBN 978-1-4342-1368-6 (pbk.)
        [1. Superheroes—Fiction.] I. Doescher, Erik, ill. II. Title.
PZ7.H67127Po 2009
[Fic]—dc22   2008032478

Summary: When animals and people begin to disappear in one of Gotham
City's parks, Batman suspects that the deadly Poison Ivy and her creepy
plants are at work again. But the green villainess is locked behind bars.
Batman goes to investigate, and just in the nick of time. When he arrives
at the park, he sees a police officer dragged into the depths of the sewer
system. The officer was pulled there by living vines!

Art Director: Bob Lentz
Designer: Brann Garvey

1 2 3 4 5 6 14 13 12 11 10 09

TABLE of CONTENTS

CHAPTER 1

NO BUGS 4

CHAPTER 2

THE ATTACK 10

CHAPTER 3

POISON IVY 20

CHAPTER 4

THE RESCUE 32

CHAPTER 5

IVY'S EXHIBIT .46

NO BUGS

Gotham City's new arboretum brought many visitors to Robinson Park. People came to see the new garden's brightly colored flowers and strange exotic plants. That's why Carter Garvey and his mom were there. At least, that was his mom's reason for visiting the park.

Carter had other plans. He agreed to tag along only because he was interested in insects. The garden's unusual plants were sure to attract some weird creepy-crawlies.

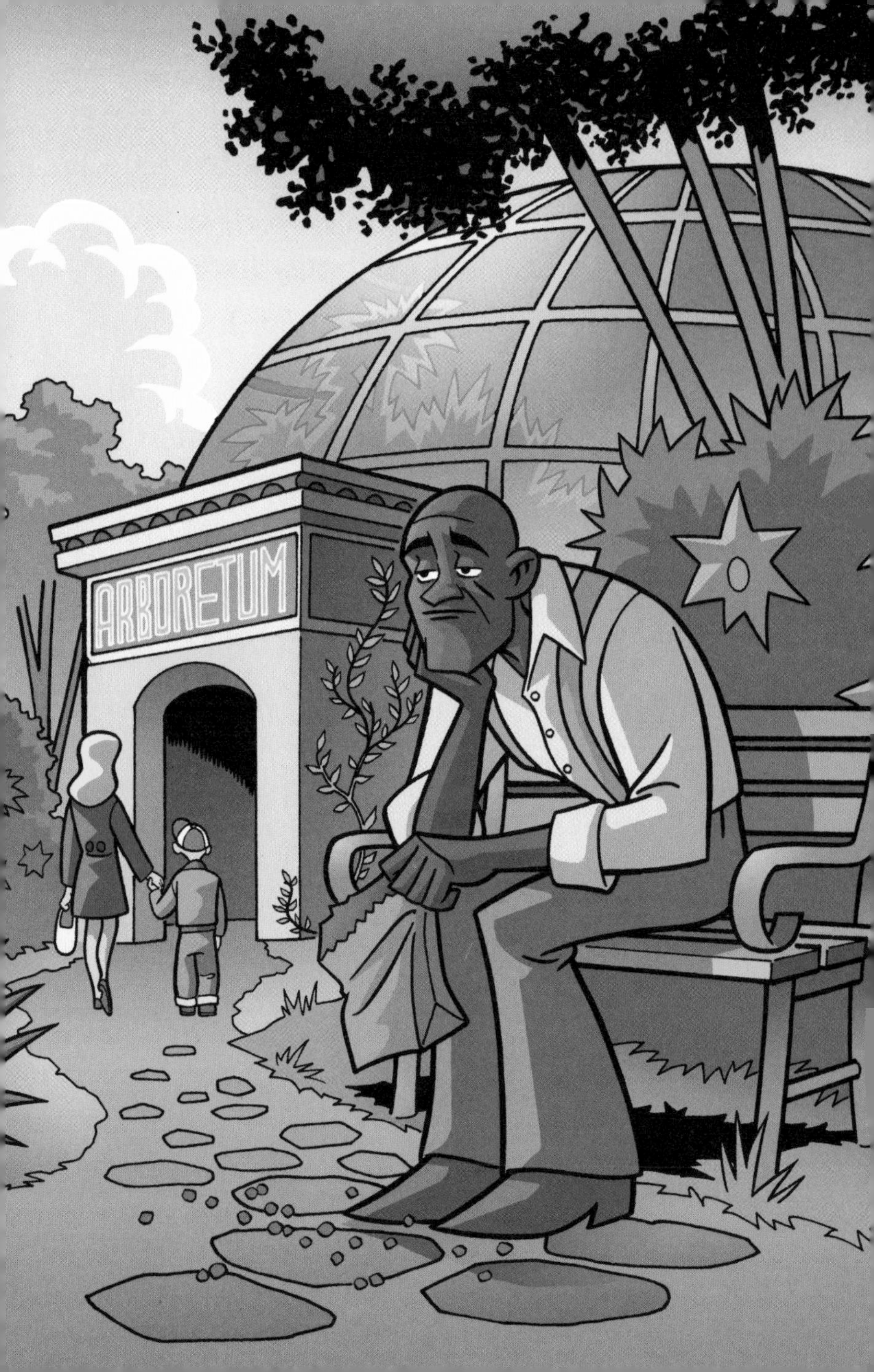
ARBORETUM

As Carter and his mom walked across the park, they saw an old man sitting alone on a bench near the front gate. The man held a greasy paper bag. He had thrown popcorn on the grass at his feet. He looked sad as he glanced from the white kernels to the empty sky above.

"What's wrong with him?" Carter asked.

"He's feeding the birds," said his Mom.

"But there aren't any birds," Carter said, looking around. "At least not here. What do you think happened to them?"

His mom stopped. She looked from the old man to Carter. "They're fine," she said. "Now, come on! There's a line forming."

Once inside the arboretum, his mom oohed and aahed over the exotic flowers and odd plants on display.

Carter lagged behind. His interests were elsewhere. He had hoped that all the weird plants meant he'd find some bizarre insects.

Carter looked and looked, but no bees buzzed from flower to flower. No butterflies colored the sky. Not so much as an ant crawled across the ground.

When he saw his mom talking to one of the park's gardeners, he ran over to them.

"Ah, this young man must be your son," the gardener said.

"Yes, though, I think he likes bugs better than plants," his mom said.

"Yeah, and why aren't there any insects here, mister?" Carter interrupted.

"Carter!" his mom snapped. "Can't you ask politely?"

"It's a good question," the gardener said. "The arboretum doesn't have insects because the plants are self-pollinating."

Carter had learned in school that some plants could pollinate themselves. But most types needed insects or animals to carry their pollen from one plant to another.

That's strange, thought Carter. He didn't remember seeing any animals in the park either. No squirrels. No birds. Nothing.

Billionaire Bruce Wayne had been watching Carter. Why was the boy digging through plants, brushing aside leaves, and turning over rocks? The boy seemed bothered that he couldn't find something.

When Carter ran over to one of the gardeners, Wayne had followed. He quietly hid behind the gardener and listened.

The explanation for the missing insects struck Wayne as odd. Just like Carter, the billionaire felt something was wrong. But unlike Carter, the billionaire was going to investigate further. Secretly, Bruce Wayne was Gotham City's greatest hero: Batman. He turned and headed toward the exit.

"Oh, Mr. Wayne!" a woman called out.

Wayne looked back. The manager of the arboretum was running toward him.

"Mr. Wayne, you haven't seen the banquet hall," she said. "Are you still interested in holding your company's party here?"

"Sorry, not this year," he apologized. He turned and exited the arboretum.

Something about this place bugs me, Wayne thought.

CHAPTER 2

THE ATTACK

At sunset, the old man sitting near the arboretum got off the park bench. For thirty years he had fed the pigeons in Robinson Park. Every day they flocked to him for bread crumbs, potato chips, or popcorn. Today, however, the pigeons never came.

As the man walked along the wall of bushes encircling the arboretum, he saw a fluttering of wings. A bird had flown into a leafy bush. Shortly afterward, he heard frightened cries.

The old man rushed over to the bush. The bird was gone. All that remained were a few feathers caught in the crook of some branches.

The leaves started to rustle. Something snaked its way through the bushes.

The man stepped back, afraid. As he retreated, he tripped. A vine had wrapped around his ankle.

He crashed to the ground.

Quickly, the old man got on his hands and knees. He began to crawl away.

More vines shot out from the bushes. They twisted around his arms, waist, and legs. Their deadly grip grew tighter.

He couldn't move.

The old man felt himself being pulled back toward the bushes. As he tried to scream, a vine wrapped around his mouth.

Then suddenly, a sharp metal object sliced through the air. *Schinggggg* The vines were cut. They loosened their grip.

Batman's shadowy figure stood over the man. He reached down and pulled the man to his feet. Then he reached down and picked up the metal weapon, a Batarang.

More vines shot out from the bushes. They seized Batman's wrists and ankles. They twisted around his legs and arms.

"Run!" Batman yelled at the man.

The Batarang, reflecting the moon's silver light, moved in Batman's hands. With a quick flick of his wrists, he freed himself from the vines.

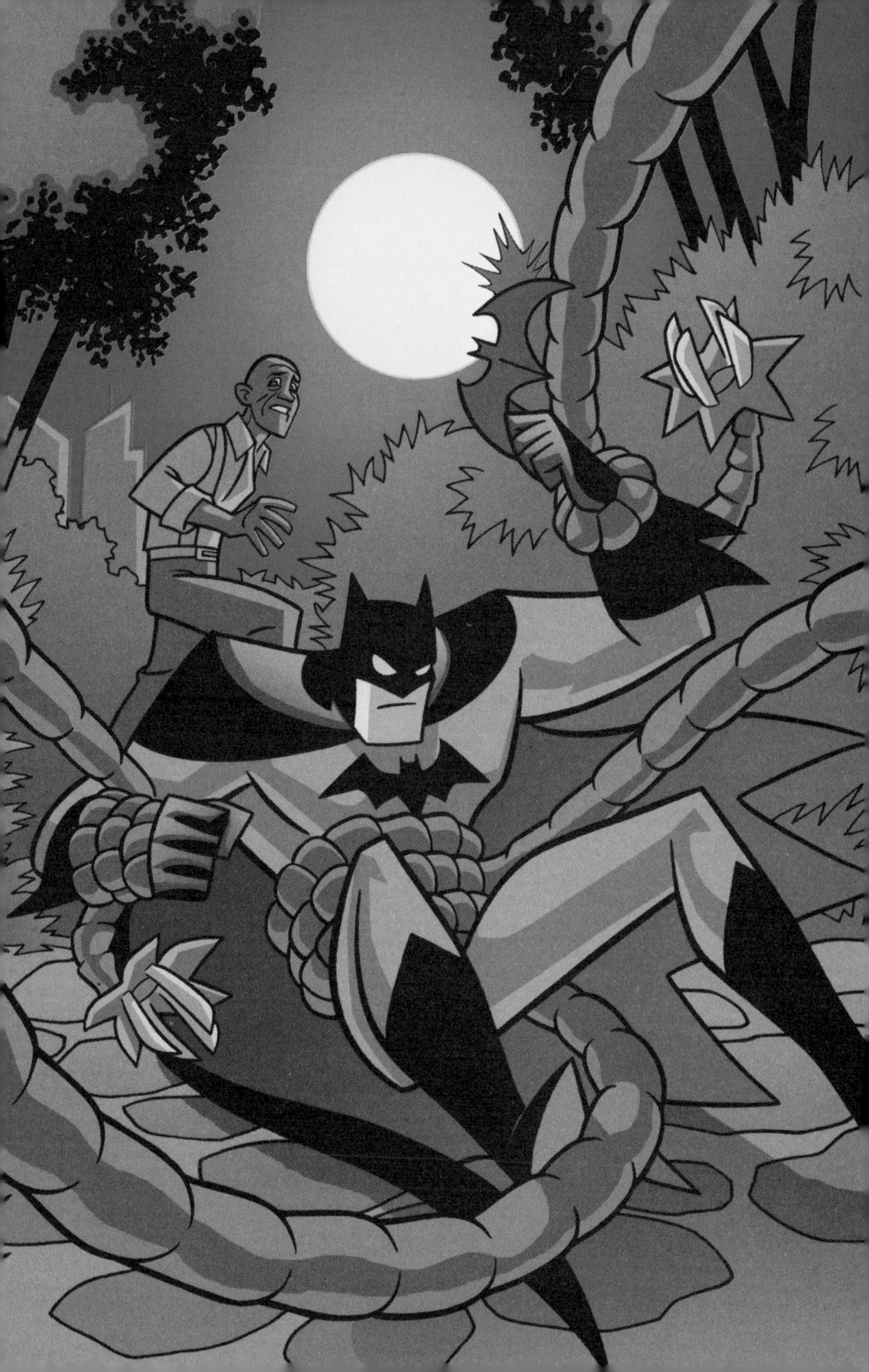

Still, more vines attacked. Batman leaped aside, swiftly slicing the vines before they could reach him. **F***zzt!* **F***zzt!*

Then, as suddenly as they had appeared, the vines were gone. Batman searched everywhere. He looked in the bushes. He walked around the arboretum. But he couldn't find the source of the vines. They had completely vanished.

"Alfred," Batman spoke into his headset. Alfred worked as Bruce Wayne's butler and Batman's trusted assistant. "Patch me through to Commissioner Gordon."

Moments later, the police chief's voice rang in Batman's headset. "What's wrong, Batman?" he asked.

"A man was attacked in Robinson Park," Batman replied.

"Did you catch the attacker?" asked the commissioner.

"No, but the victim is safe," Batman said, looking at the frightened old man.

"I can send a squad car down to assist you," Gordon said, "if you need help searching for the assailant."

"We may need more than a few police officers. I think the park should be closed," Batman said. "I'm not exactly sure what attacked the man. It's not safe here."

"Mayor Hill would never agree to that. The annual Mayor's Banquet is this weekend. It's being held at the arboretum," the commissioner explained. "Leaders from major cities, like Metropolis and New York, will be here. It would be embarrassing for him to cancel now."

After Commissioner Gordon agreed to send a squad down to the arboretum, Batman called Alfred back.

"What's your next move?" Alfred asked.

Batman grabbed a piece of vine that was stuck to his Batsuit. "I think it's time to brush up on our botany."

•   •   •

Back in his secret hideout, the Batcave, Batman slouched in his chair. He was studying the cross section of a leaf that was displayed on a large computer screen in front of him.

Alfred walked up behind Batman. He set a cup of tea down next to the Caped Crusader. "Any luck identifying those creepy vines?" he asked.

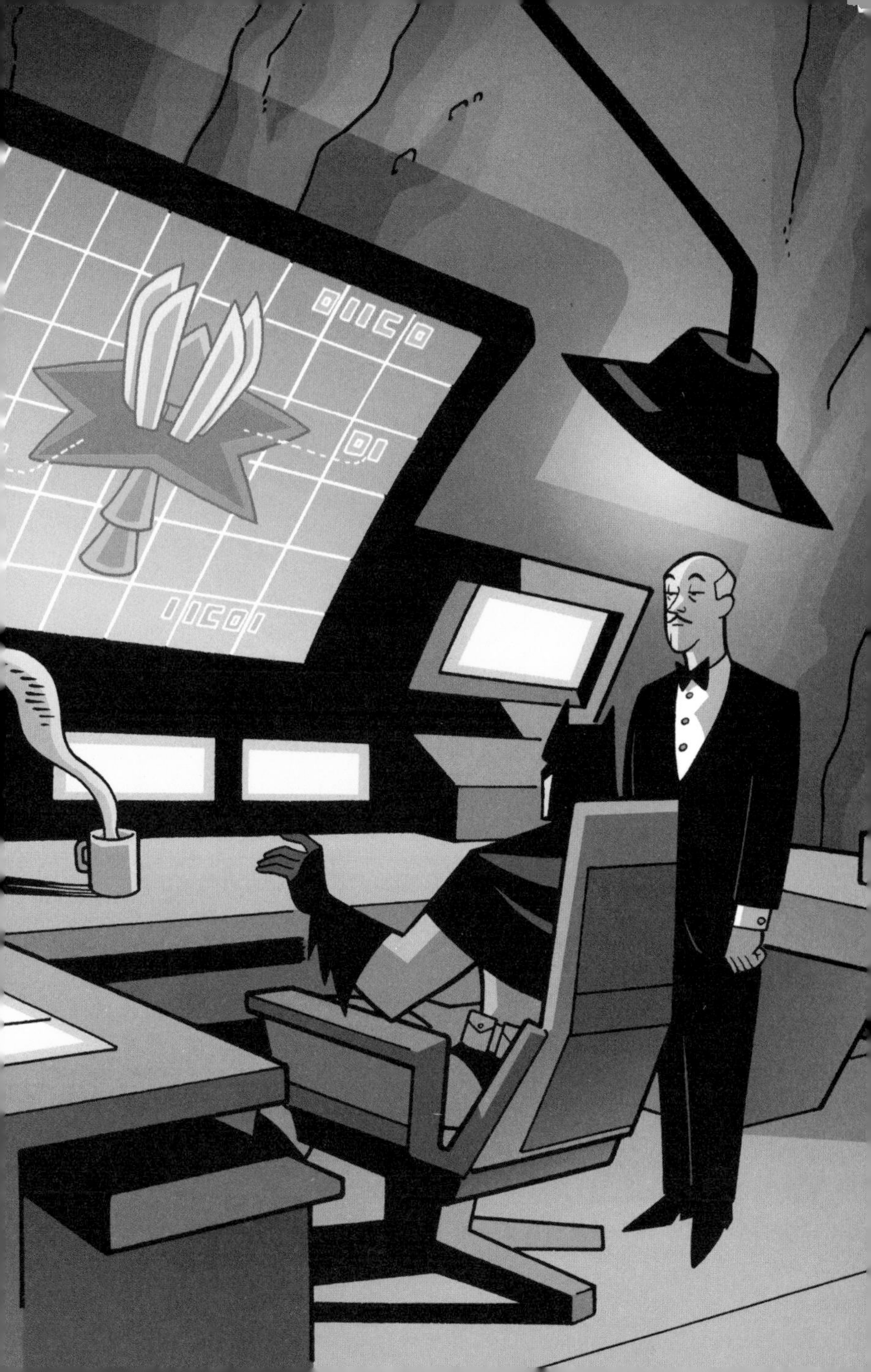

"None," Batman replied. "They don't match any of the plants at the park. And there's nothing on file that matches either."

"But I've learned that they are some sort of carnivorous, or meat-eating, plant," Batman continued. He pointed to the computer screen. "See those spines on the leaf? They're for holding onto prey. Instead of getting nutrients from soil, these vines eat whatever they catch."

"Might that include cats and dogs as well as insects and birds, sir?" Alfred asked.

Batman spun around in his chair to face Alfred. "Yes," said Batman. "Why do you ask?"

"Commissioner Gordon e-mailed a list of missing pet reports," Alfred replied.

"Let me guess," Batman interrupted. "The disappearances are centered around the arboretum."

"It appears so," Alfred said.

Batman stood up and walked toward the Batcave's elevator.

"Where are you headed?" Alfred asked.

"To visit our local plant expert," Batman replied. "If anyone knows about these vile vines, it's her."

CHAPTER 3

POISON IVY

Batman sped toward Arkham Asylum on his Batcycle. He was headed to see Pamela Isley, better known as Poison Ivy. She had been locked up at the asylum.

Not only was she a famed botanist, she was also a deadly villain. She had vowed to protect all plant life on earth, even if laws were broken and people were harmed.

Before entering her Plexiglas cell, a guard gave Batman an oxygen mask to wear. Poison Ivy could exhale toxic fumes.

Her cell's special air system kept the fumes from spreading through the asylum. The guards and other inmates were safe. But others going into her cell needed an oxygen mask, or she could poison them.

Poison Ivy jumped up as Batman entered her cell. "Batman, you came to visit," she said, smiling. "How sweet, since you're the one who had me locked up."

"This isn't a social call," said Batman.

"With you, it never is," Poison Ivy said, frowning. "All you care about is solving crimes."

"I'm here to find out what you know about the new arboretum," Batman said.

"It's full of plants," Poison Ivy teased. "If you let me out, we could go there. I'd even teach you all of their scientific names."

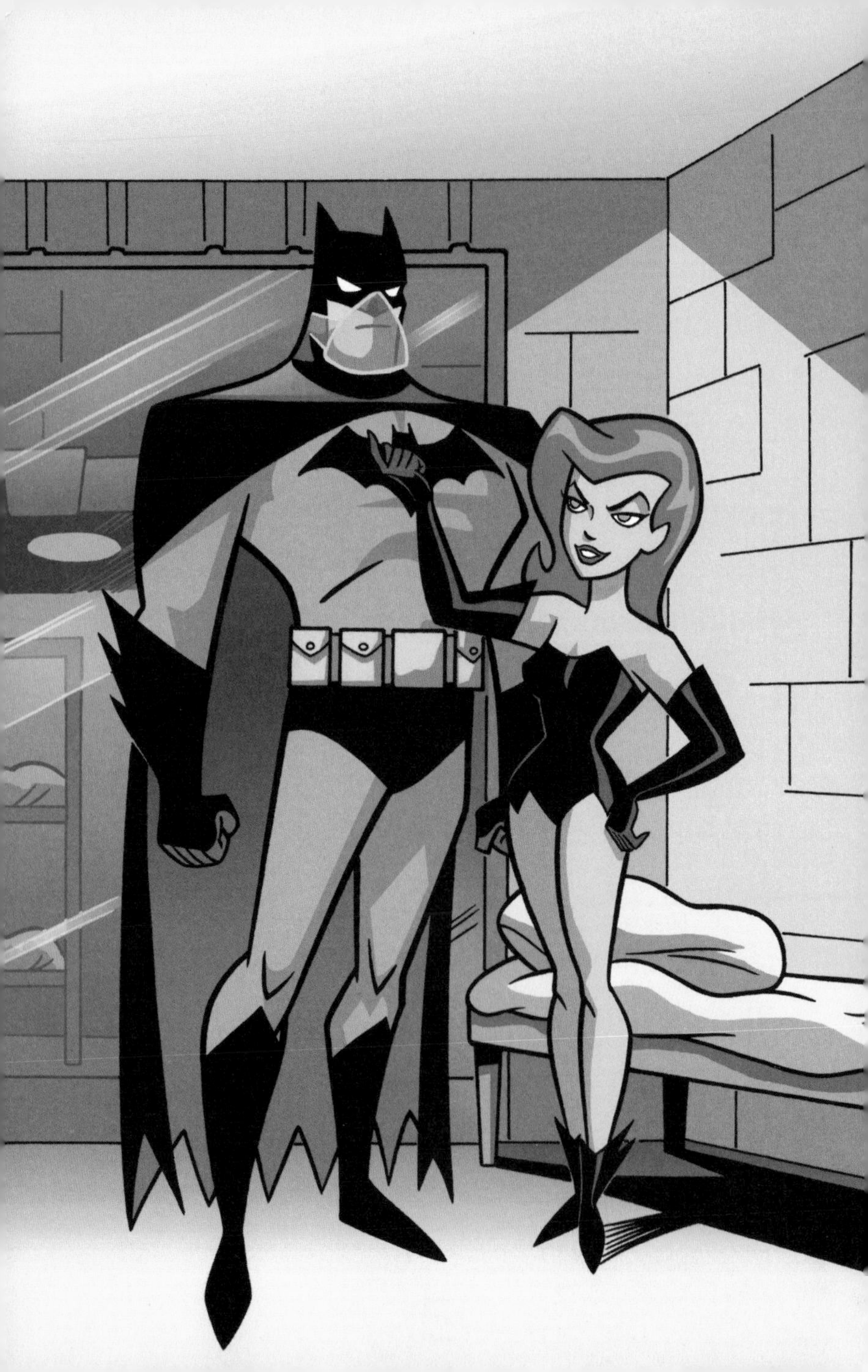

"In other words," said Batman, "you want me to help you escape."

"Escape? Why would I escape? I have everything I need here," Poison Ivy said. "Fresh air. Bright lights. And the rotten food they serve is perfect for compost."

Poison Ivy smiled. "Besides, I've put down roots here. This is home sweet home."

Batman turned to leave. "Where are you going?" Poison Ivy asked, looking confused.

"To the arboretum," Batman replied. "I have all the information I need."

After leaving her cell, Batman told the guard to keep an eye on Poison Ivy. "Call Commissioner Gordon if she does anything unusual," Batman said.

"Everything about her is unusual," the guard joked.

Outside the asylum, the streets were quiet and empty. The Batcycle's engine roared, breaking the silence. Batman sped south, toward Robinson Park. He hoped he could reach the arboretum before anyone else was attacked.

As he raced around a corner, Batman radioed Alfred. "Why are you heading back there?" Alfred asked.

"I'm looking for roots," Batman replied.

"Roots?" asked Alfred, puzzled.

"Yes, it was something Poison Ivy said," Batman replied. "I think the plant I'm after is hidden underground."

A few miles away, Gotham Police Officer Renee Montoya stood at the arboretum's front gate. She had called the manager an hour ago, but the woman never showed up.

A slight breeze rustled the bushes. Renee shivered. Not because it was a cool night, but because this place gave her the creeps. It was quiet. Too quiet. No crickets chirped. There weren't any moths fluttering around the street lamp near the gate. Even the bats seemed to stay clear of this place.

All except one. "Officer Montoya," a voice spoke from the shadows.

Renee whirled around, fists in front of her. She was ready to fight.

Batman stepped out of the darkness. "I didn't know Commissioner Gordon sent you down here," he said.

Renee relaxed. "He couldn't convince Mayor Hill to close the park on your word," she said. "So he sent me and my partner, Detective Ben Harper, to investigate."

Renee pointed to where her partner had been standing. He was gone. Just then, a cry split the night. **AAAAAHHH!**

"That must be Ben!" Renee shouted.

They ran toward the scream. Up ahead in the moonlight, Batman saw Harper tangled in vines. They were pulling him through the bushes, into the arboretum.

"Renee, head around to the front entrance," Batman commanded.

"How will you get in?" Renee asked.

Batman touched his Utility Belt. A Batarang attached to a thin wire sprang into his hand. Batman tossed the Batarang at a tree limb hanging over the bushes. It looped securely around a branch. Then, Batman leaped into the air, swinging over the hedge of bushes.

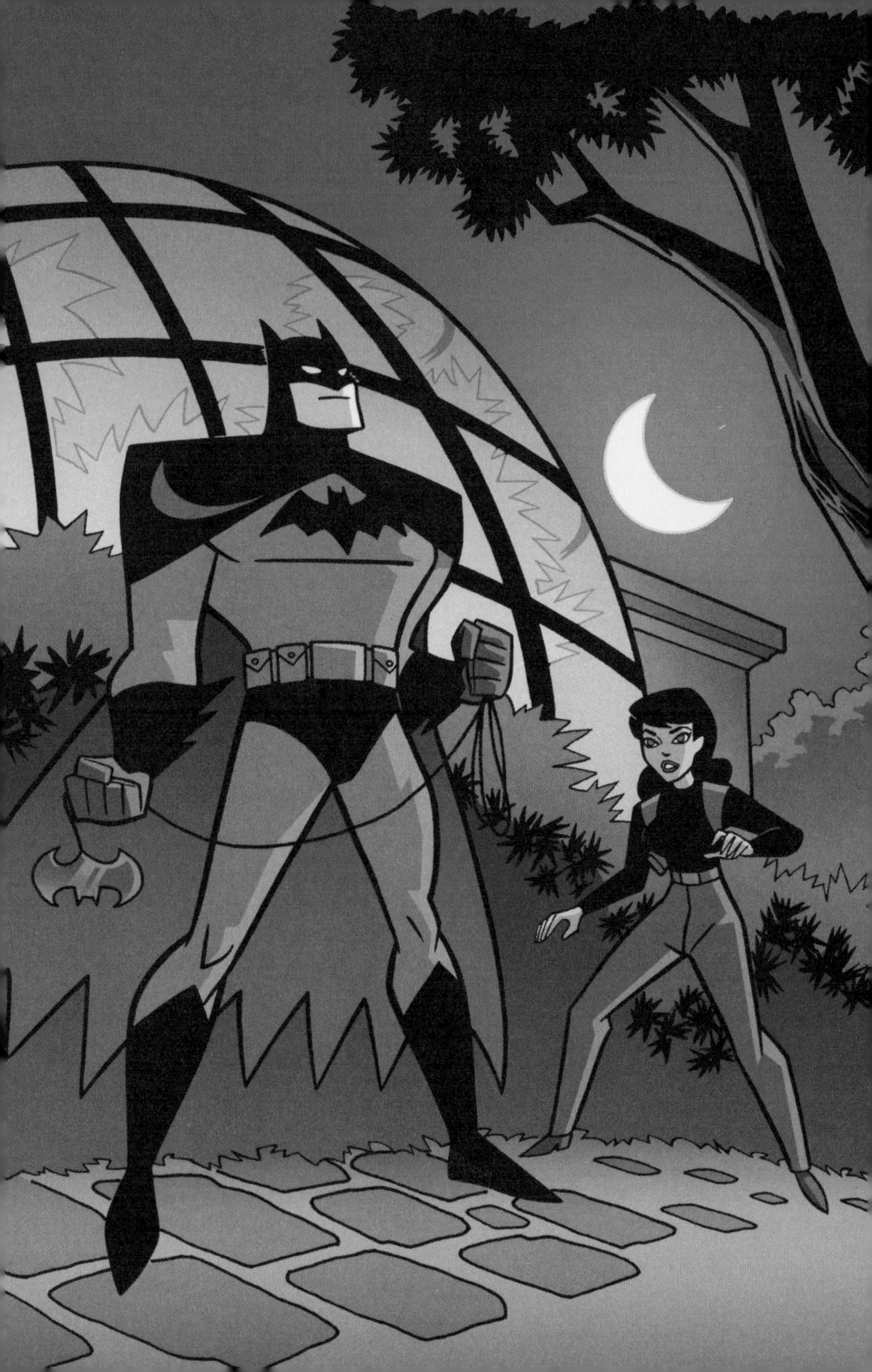

"Never mind," Renee said as she headed back toward the arboretum's entrance.

Batman landed with a heavy thud. In front of him, he saw the vines dragging Harper across the ground. They were pulling him into the center of the arboretum, toward the banquet hall.

As Batman stepped forward, thick vines sprung up all around. Their snaky tendrils surrounded him.

Batman grabbed a small spray canister from his Utility Belt. It contained a yellowish liquid that he had created. It would protect him against Poison Ivy's plants. As he squirted a yellow mist at the vines, they shriveled and shrank away.

Harper was no longer in sight. He had been dragged off by the vines.

Batman rushed forward. In the distance, he saw the arboretum's banquet hall. It was a large glass building that looked like a greenhouse. The doors were wide open. Above them was a banner that read "Welcome to the 10th Annual Mayor's Banquet."

What if the mayor had been here when the vines attacked? Batman thought. *That must have been Poison Ivy's plan.*

Batman sprinted through the banquet hall doorway. In the middle of the hall was a gaping hole where a dance floor had once been. Detective Harper was nowhere to be seen.

Batman looked down into the dark depths of the hole. Renee ran up to him. "Where's Ben?" she asked, frightened.

"Down there," Batman replied. "If my guess is correct, that hole opens into the Gotham sewer system and leads back to Arkham Asylum."

From below, a muffled cry could be heard. Batman and Renee looked down into the hole. They knew who the screams were coming from.

Renee was about to leap into the hole. Batman grabbed her arm.

"It's too dangerous," he said.

"I have to save my partner," she replied.

"I'll go after Harper," Batman told her. "I need you to make sure Poison Ivy doesn't escape from Arkham Asylum. This plant is one of hers."

With that, Batman jumped into the hole. He fell into darkness.

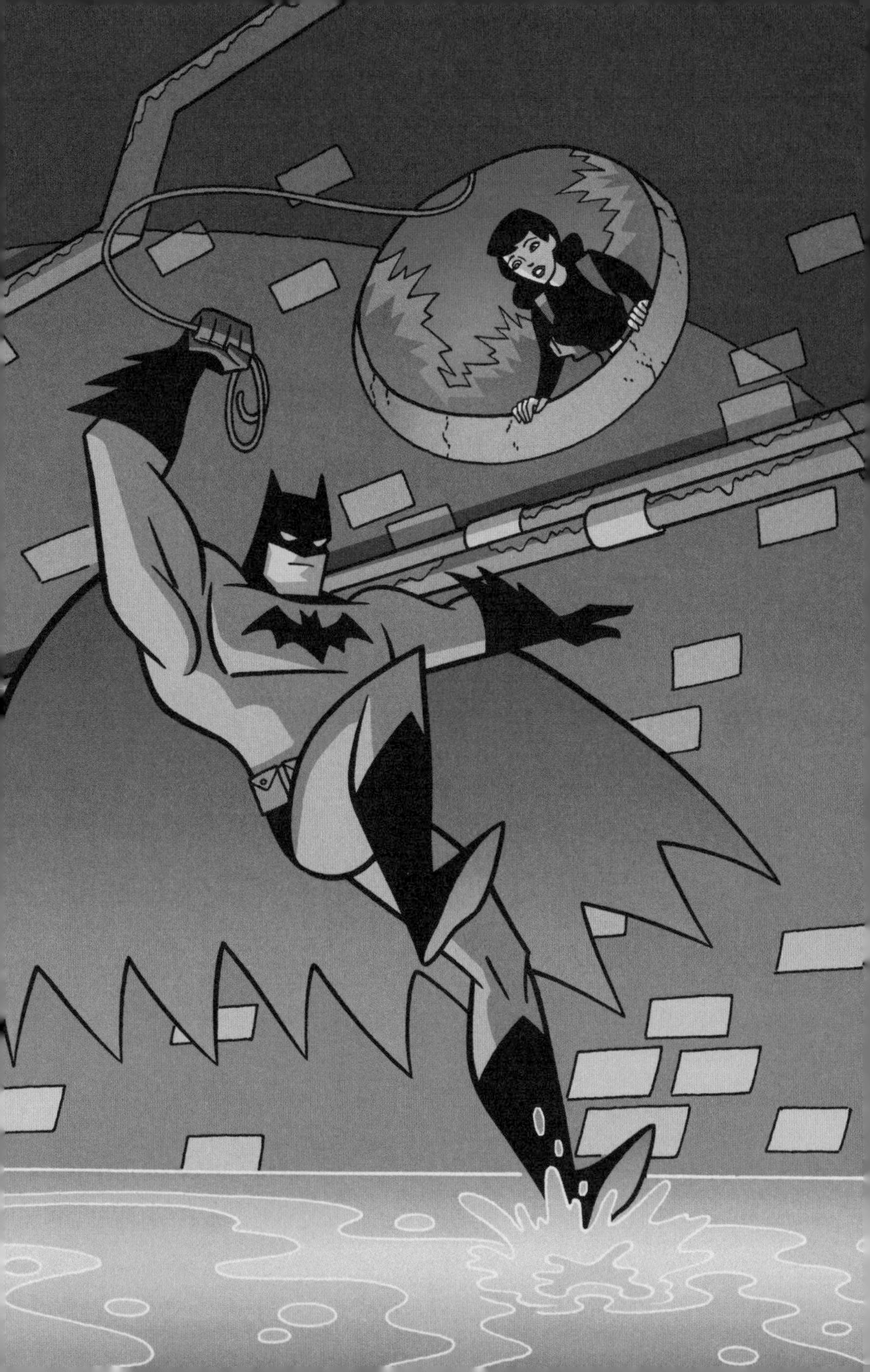

CHAPTER 4

THE RESCUE

SPLASH! Batman landed in a pool of water. He grabbed a flashlight from his Utility Belt and clicked it on. The tunnel stretched out before him into the darkness. From far away, he could hear muffled scraping noises.

Batman raced down the tunnel, ducking under pipes and jumping over puddles. He wasn't sure where he was going. Every once in a while he stopped and listened. As soon as he heard Harper's muffled cries for help, he would head off in their direction.

He knew he was getting closer. The cries were growing louder.

Then he found himself in an area where several tunnels branched off. He didn't know which one to follow. The sounds of splashing and the cries for help echoed from every direction.

Batman radioed Alfred. "Patch me through to Officer Montoya."

"One moment," Alfred replied.

A few seconds later, Batman heard Renee's voice in his headset. "This is Officer Montoya," she said.

"Are you at the asylum yet?" Batman asked.

"I'm just crossing the Sprang River now," she replied.

"Contact me as soon as you reach Poison Ivy's cell," Batman said.

"Have you found Harper?" Renee asked.

"Not yet, but I'm close," Batman replied.

Batman thought for a moment. He wasn't sure which tunnel to follow. There was a manhole cover above him. He quickly climbed up and opened it.

Overhead, the stars were barely visible through the glow of Gotham City's neon lights. But one star, Polaris, still shined brightly.

That gives me an idea, Batman thought.

Polaris was found at the end of the little dipper's handle. It was also called the North Star because it was above Earth's North Pole. Long ago, sailors had used the star to tell which direction was north.

Returning to the sewer, Batman picked the tunnel that was in the same direction as the North Star. Arkham Asylum was north of Robinson Park.

Soon, Batman could hear Harper's cries again. He was getting close. After racing down a few more tunnels, Batman turned a corner and skidded to a stop.

The tunnel opened into a large, dark cavern. The light from his flashlight dimly lit the far wall. The tunnel he was in was the only one he could see exiting the cavern.

Batman took a few cautious steps forward. CRUNCH! CRUNCH!

Something hard crunched under his foot. Looking down, he noticed it was a white bone, picked clean of meat.

Shining his flashlight across the cavern floor, Batman saw that it was covered in animal skeletons. Birds. Cats. Dogs.

"Help!" Batman heard Harper cry.

Batman shined the light above him. What he saw both amazed and horrified him. Hundreds of vines dangled from a large pipe in the ceiling. One extremely thick vine was pulling Harper toward the pipe. Batman couldn't imagine what was inside the pipe. But he knew it couldn't be good, at least not for Harper.

Batman aimed and tossed a Batarang.

Schingggg!

It sliced through the thick vine. Harper fell and landed safely in the pile of bones. As soon as he crashed to the ground, other vines swarmed over him.

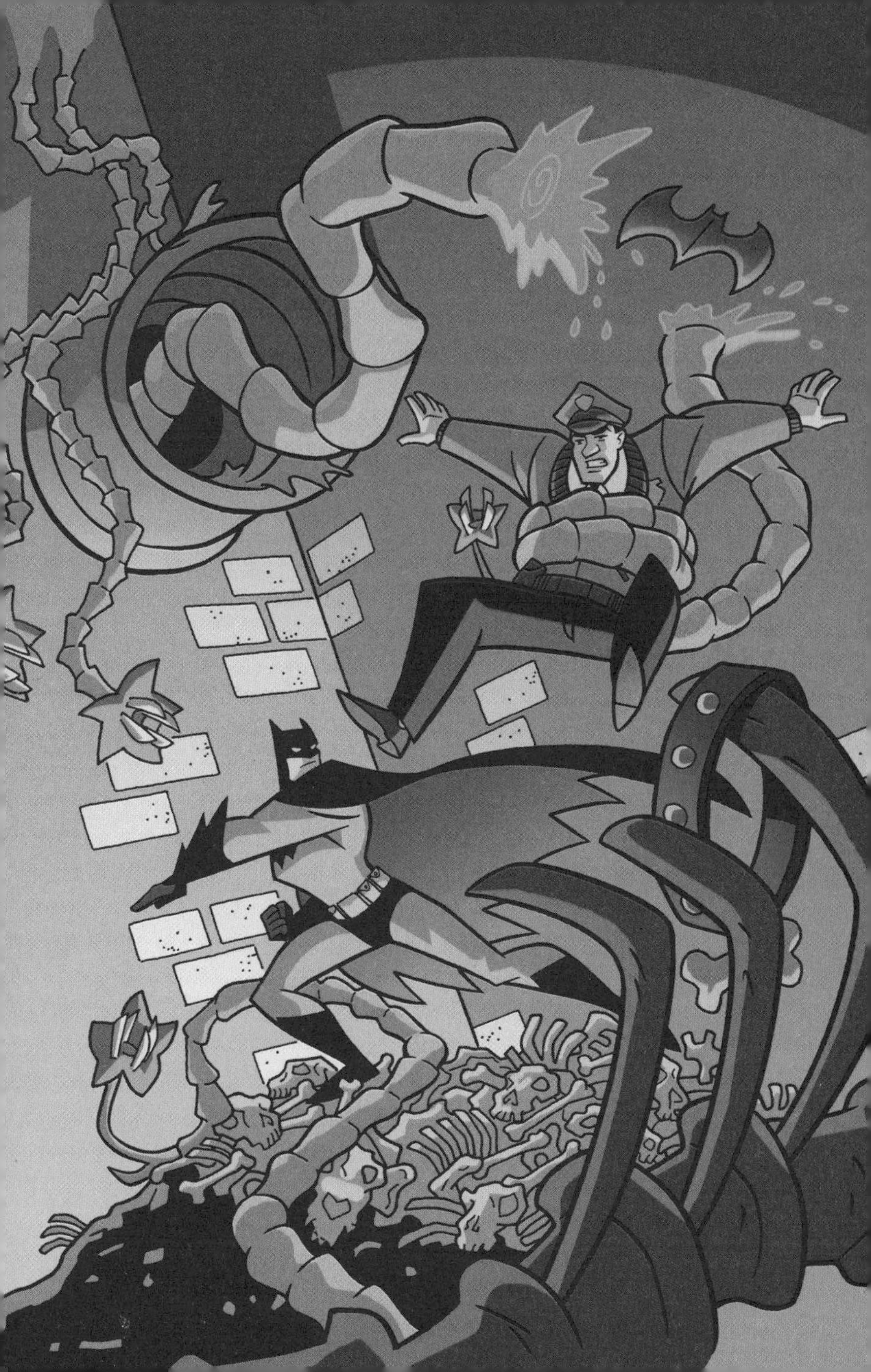

Batman tried to reach the detective, but there were too many vines. His spray canister quickly ran out of yellowish liquid. His remaining Batarangs weren't enough to cut the vines tangling Harper.

The vines began to attack Batman as well. Batman backed out of the cavern. He used his Batarangs to slice any vines that came near him.

As he fought the writhing tendrils, Batman heard Alfred's voice on his headset. "Is everything all right, sir?" Alfred asked.

Just then, a vine wrapped around Batman's waist. "I'm a bit tangled up at the moment," Batman replied.

He cut through the vine, freeing himself. Others quickly slithered toward him. He dodged away from them.

"Officer Montoya would like to speak with you," Alfred said.

"Put her through," Batman replied as he slashed at more vines.

"I'm here with Poison Ivy," Renee said.

A creeper twisted around Batman's ankle. He fell to the ground. *Oomf!*

"Tell Poison Ivy," Batman began, "if she doesn't stop her plant, we'll have to kill it."

Moments later, Officer Montoya spoke again. "She says your threats won't work with her," said Renee. "You'll have to let her out of the asylum first."

Batman tried to cut the vine around his ankle, but another one twisted around his wrist. He dropped his Batarang. The vine quickly slithered up his arm and wrapped around his neck.

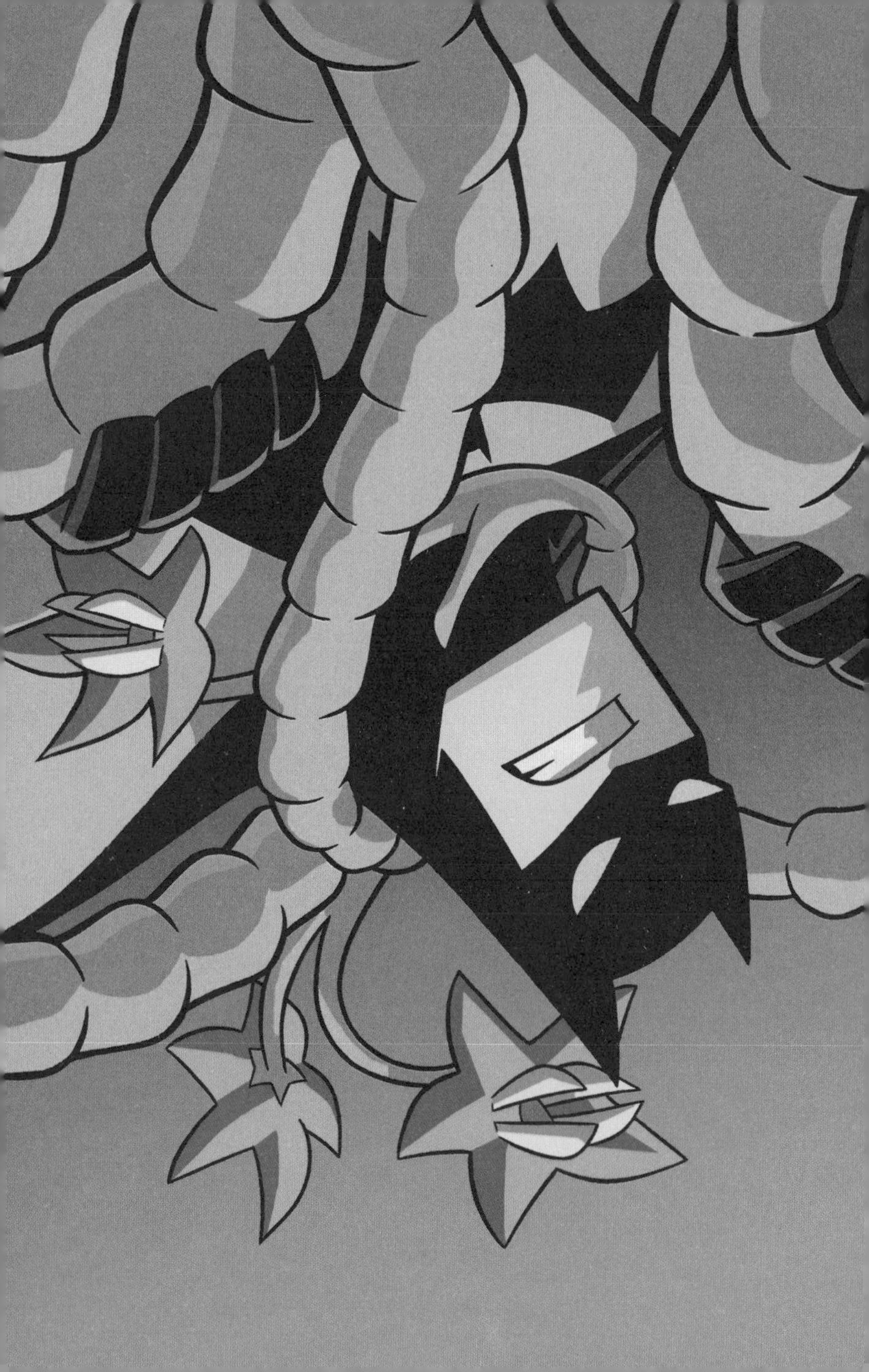

"Tell her," Batman yelled, "if she doesn't stop her plant, not only will we have to kill it, but people will be afraid to visit the arboretum. It will close. All of the plants there will die as well."

Batman grabbed onto the tunnel wall. He tried to stop from being pulled back into the cavern.

"People will stop going to Robinson Park," Batman continued. "It will close as well and be turned into a parking lot."

He listened for a reply from his headset.

Silence.

Then Batman felt the vines lift him off the ground. He was being carried toward the pipe. From the corner of his eye, he could see Harper dangling from some vines above him.

"You win," came Renee's response through Batman's headset. "But Ivy says you have to promise not to destroy her plant. It's special."

"All right," Batman managed to say before a vine wrapped around his mouth.

At the asylum, Poison Ivy walked over to the sink in her cell. She reached her hands into its basin. When Renee walked over to see what Poison Ivy was doing, she noticed something odd. Roots were extending from the sink's drain.

Poison Ivy nodded toward the security cameras in her cell. "I usually turn on the water. The guards just think that I'm washing my hands."

The roots wiggled out of the drain and wrapped around Poison Ivy's wrists.

"I developed a special seed right before I was locked up," Poison Ivy explained. "I smuggled it into the asylum with me. I was able to grow the seed in the sink. Its roots extend from the asylum's plumbing system into the city's sewers.

"What makes this plant special," she continued, "is that it reacts to the chemicals in my body. The chemicals that make me the way I am. If I use the right mixture, I can send it a message to let go of its prey."

Back in the cavern, the vines suddenly loosened their grip. Batman crashed to the ground. A moment later, Harper landed next to him. The vines stopped moving.

"Batman," Renee's voice spoke into Batman's headset. "She did it. Is Ben safe?"

Batman looked over at Harper, lying in a pile of crushed animal bones. He looked like he was in shock.

"No broken bones," Batman replied. "Well, at least none that belong to him."

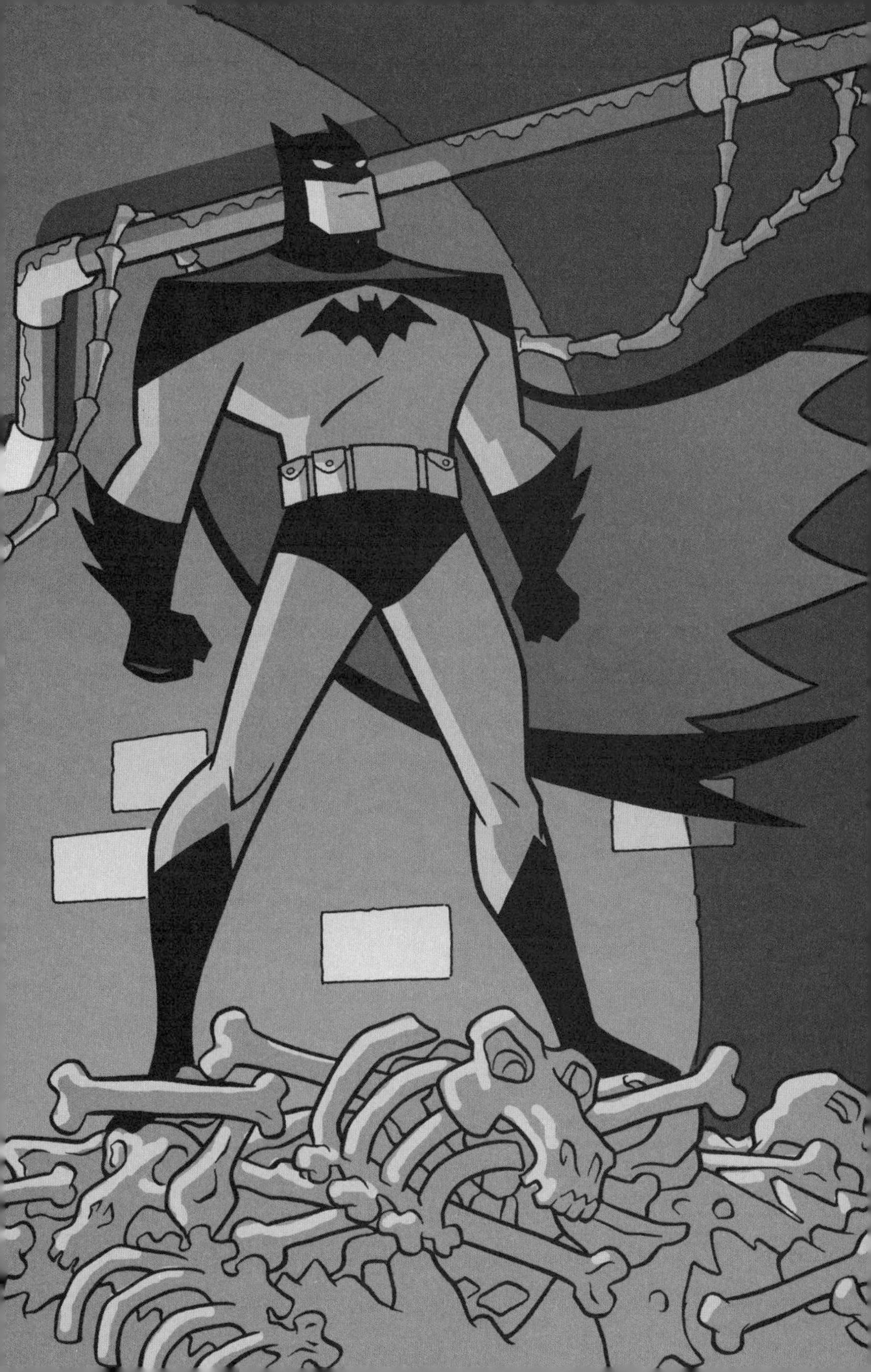

CHAPTER 5

IVY'S EXHIBIT

A few weeks later, billionaire Bruce Wayne and his butler, Alfred, stood in front of a new display at the arboretum. In the center of a stone patio sat a large, empty flowerpot. At least, it looked empty.

Thick wire netting surrounded the patio. Metal railings held back the crowd of people that had gathered near the exhibit.

"Do you really think it's safe to have Poison Ivy's plant on display, sir?" asked Alfred. "Especially after we learned that the gardeners here were helping her."

"They didn't help her willingly," Bruce replied. "The workers were afraid of Poison Ivy and what she might do to them if they didn't aid her.

"All they were doing was taking care of her plant," Bruce continued. "They didn't know Poison Ivy planned to use it to kidnap the city mayors. Or that she wanted to hold the mayors hostage unless she was freed from Arkham Asylum."

Bruce added, "I promised that her plant wouldn't be destroyed."

"I still don't like it," Alfred scowled.

Bruce motioned to the empty-looking pot. "We only saved a small clipping from the original plant. Poison Ivy said as long as it wasn't overfed, it wouldn't outgrow its pot."

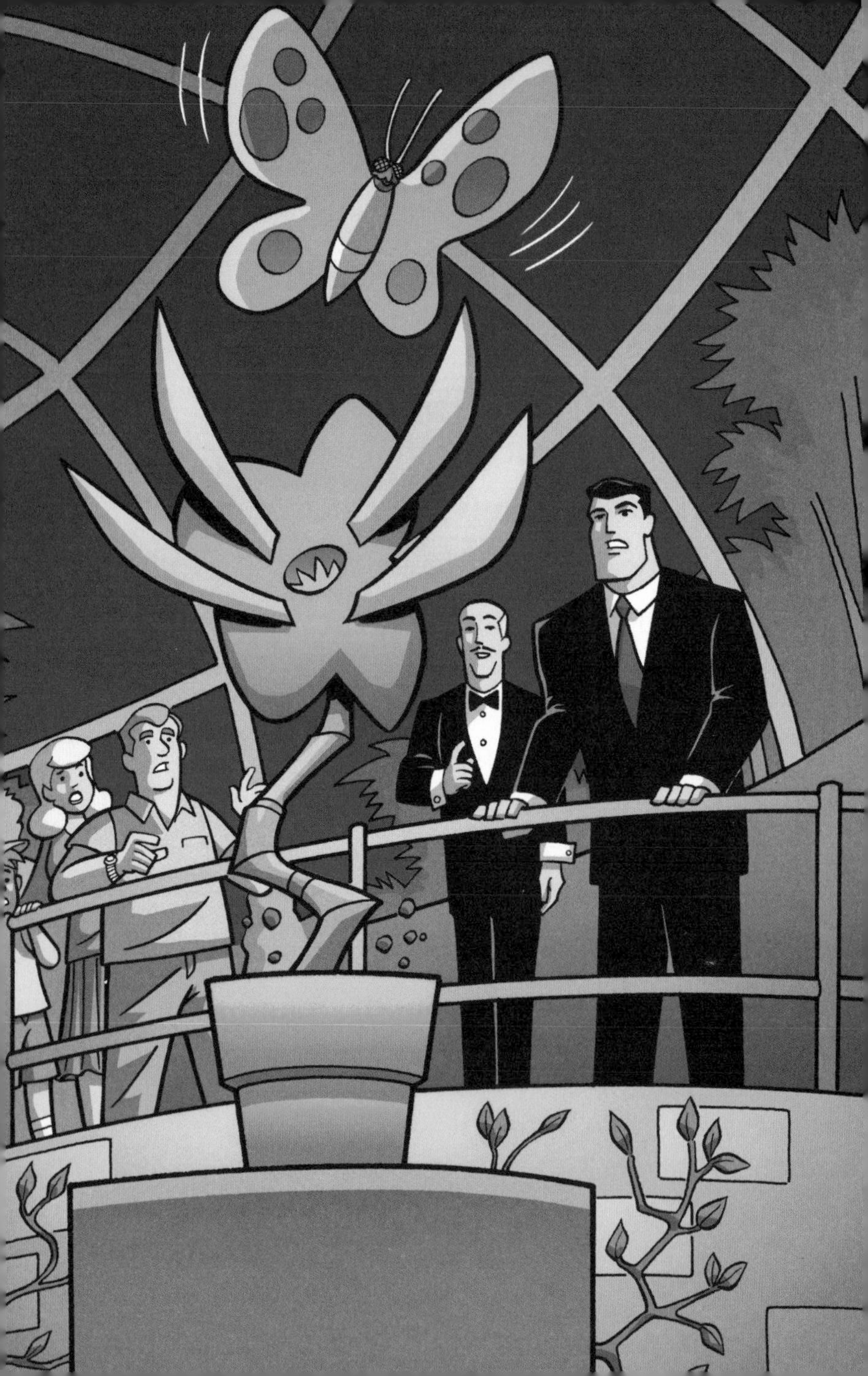

Just then, a butterfly fluttered through the wire netting. Its colorful wings flapped brightly in the sun's golden rays. As the butterfly neared the pot, a vine shot out. It wrapped tightly around the butterfly. Then, as quickly as it had appeared, the vine vanished into the pot with its meal.

The crowd oohed and aahed.

Alfred frowned.

"It's quite popular," Bruce said.

Poison Ivy

REAL NAME: Pamela Isley

OCCUPATION: Professional Criminal, Botanist

BASE: Gotham City

HEIGHT:
5 feet 6 inches

WEIGHT:
110 pounds

EYES:
Green

HAIR:
Chestnut

Born with immunities to plant toxins and poisons, Pamela Isley's love of plants began to grow like a weed at an early age. She eventually became a botanist, or plant scientist. Through reckless experimentation with various flora, Pamela Isley's skin itself has become poisonous. Her venomous lips and poisonous plant weapons present a real problem for the Dark Knight. But Ivy's most dangerous quality is her extreme love of nature — she cares more about the smallest seed than any human life.

G.C.P.D. GOTHAM CITY POLICE DEPARTMENT

- Poison Ivy was once engaged to Gotham's District Attorney, Harvey Dent, who eventually became the super-villain Two-Face! Their relationship ended when Dent built a prison on a field of wildflowers, unintentionally provoking Ivy's wrath.

- Poison Ivy emits toxic fragrances that can be harmful to humans. Whenever she is locked up in Arkham Asylum, a wall of Plexiglas must separate her from the guards to ensure their safety.

- Ivy may love her plant creations, but that love hasn't always been returned. A man-eating plant of her own design eventually became self-aware, or sentient! The thing called itself Harvest, and when it turned on Ivy, the Caped Crusader came to her rescue.

- Ivy's connection to plants is so strong that she can control them by thought alone! The control she has over her lethal plants makes her a dangerous foe for Gotham City Police — as well as the Dark Knight.

CONFIDENTIAL

BIOGRAPHIES

Blake A. Hoena grew up in central Wisconsin. Later, he moved to Minnesota to pursue a Masters of Fine Arts degree in Creative Writing from Minnesota State University, Mankato. Since graduating, Blake has written more than thirty books for children, including a series of graphic novels about two space alien brothers, Eek and Ack, who are determined to conquer Earth.

Erik Doescher is a freelance illustrator and video game designer based in Dallas, Texas. He attended the School of Visual Arts in New York City. Erik illustrated for a number of comic studios throughout the 1990s, and then moved to Texas to pursue videogame development and design. However, he has not completely given up on illustrating his favorite comic book characters.

Mike DeCarlo is a longtime contributor of comic art whose range extends from Batman and Iron Man to Bugs Bunny and Scooby-Doo. He resides in Connecticut with his wife and four children.

Lee Loughridge has been working in comics for more than 14 years. He currently lives in sunny California in a tent on the beach.

GLOSSARY

arboretum (ahr-buh-REE-tuhm)—a place where many different trees or shrubs are on display

assailant (uh-SEY-luhnt)—an attacker

asylum (uh-SYE-luhm)—a hospital for the mentally ill

bizarre (bi-ZAHR)—odd or unusual

cautious (KAW-shuhs)—trying hard to avoid mistakes or danger

compost (KOM-pohst)—a mixture of rotted leaves and other organic matter used to make soil richer

exotic (eg-ZOT-ik)—strange and unfamiliar

Utility Belt (yoo-TIL-uh-tee BELT)—Batman's belt, which holds all of his weaponry and gadgets

vile (VILE)—evil or repulsive

writhing (RITHE-ing)—twisting and turning around

DISCUSSION QUESTIONS

1. If you were Batman, would you have kept your word and let Poison Ivy's dangerous plant survive? Is it ever okay to break a promise?

2. How would the world be different if Poison Ivy's evil, meat-eating plants existed? Would you eat a plant that might want to eat you? Why or why not?

3. Bruce Wayne's secret identity is Batman. Why do you think he keeps his alter ego a secret? Would you tell anyone if you were a super hero? Who?

WRITING PROMPTS

1. Poison Ivy loves to create strange new plants. Create your own weird plant. What does it do? How does it look? Write about it. Then, draw a picture of your creation.

2. Poison Ivy really enjoys plants. A lot. What are your favorite things? Make a list of your hobbies and interests.

3. If Poison Ivy had refused to make her plants stop attacking Batman, what else could he have done to survive? Write your own ending to the story.

MORE NEW BATMAN ADVENTURES!

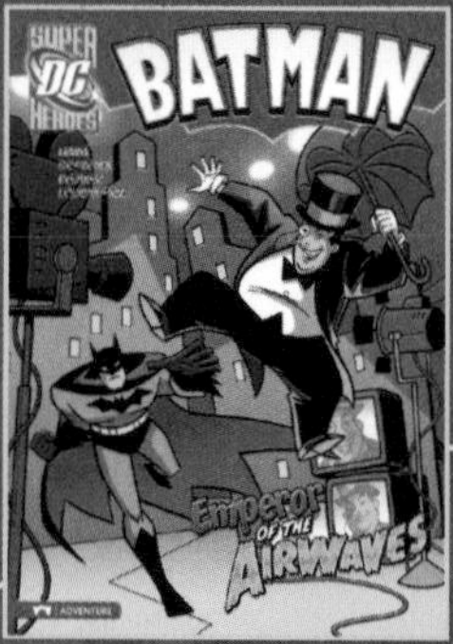
SUPER DC HEROES!
BATMAN
Emperor of the Airwaves

EMPEROR OF THE AIRWAVES

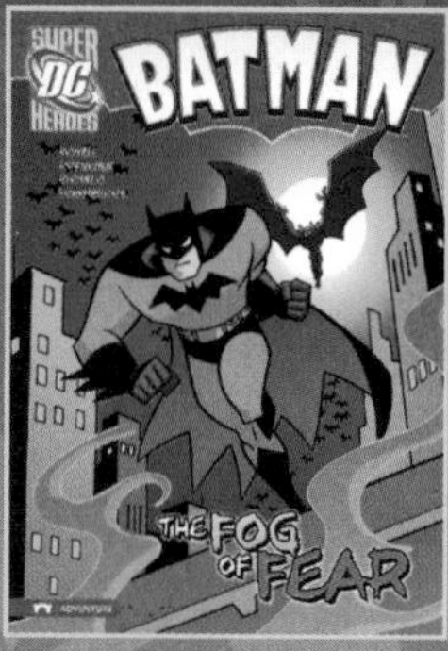
SUPER DC HEROES
BATMAN
THE FOG OF FEAR

THE FOG OF FEAR

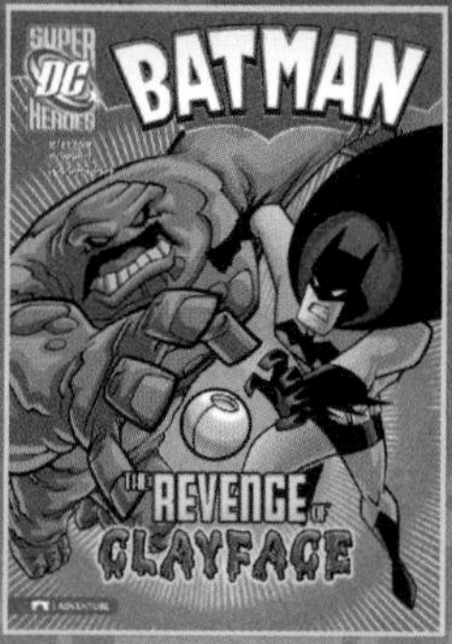
SUPER DC HEROES
BATMAN
THE REVENGE OF CLAYFACE

THE REVENGE OF CLAYFACE

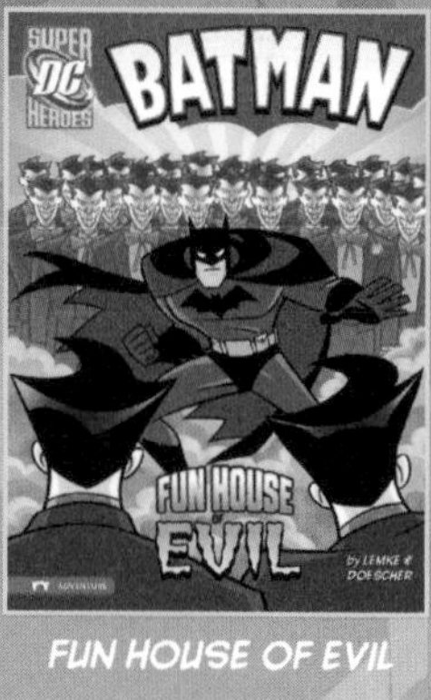
SUPER DC HEROES
BATMAN
FUN HOUSE OF EVIL
by LEMKE & DOESCHER

FUN HOUSE OF EVIL

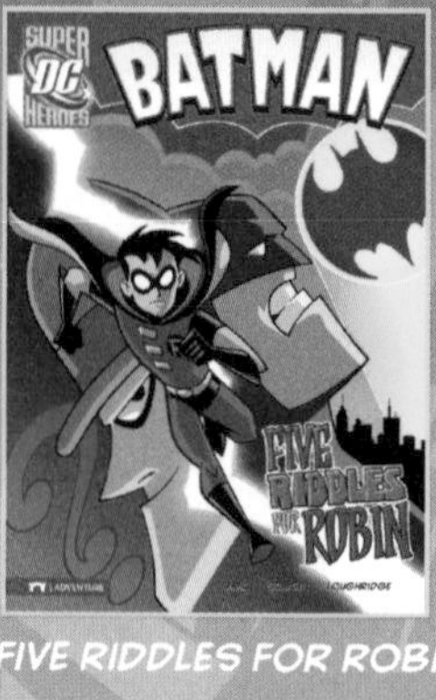
SUPER DC HEROES
BATMAN
FIVE RIDDLES FOR ROBIN

FIVE RIDDLES FOR ROBIN

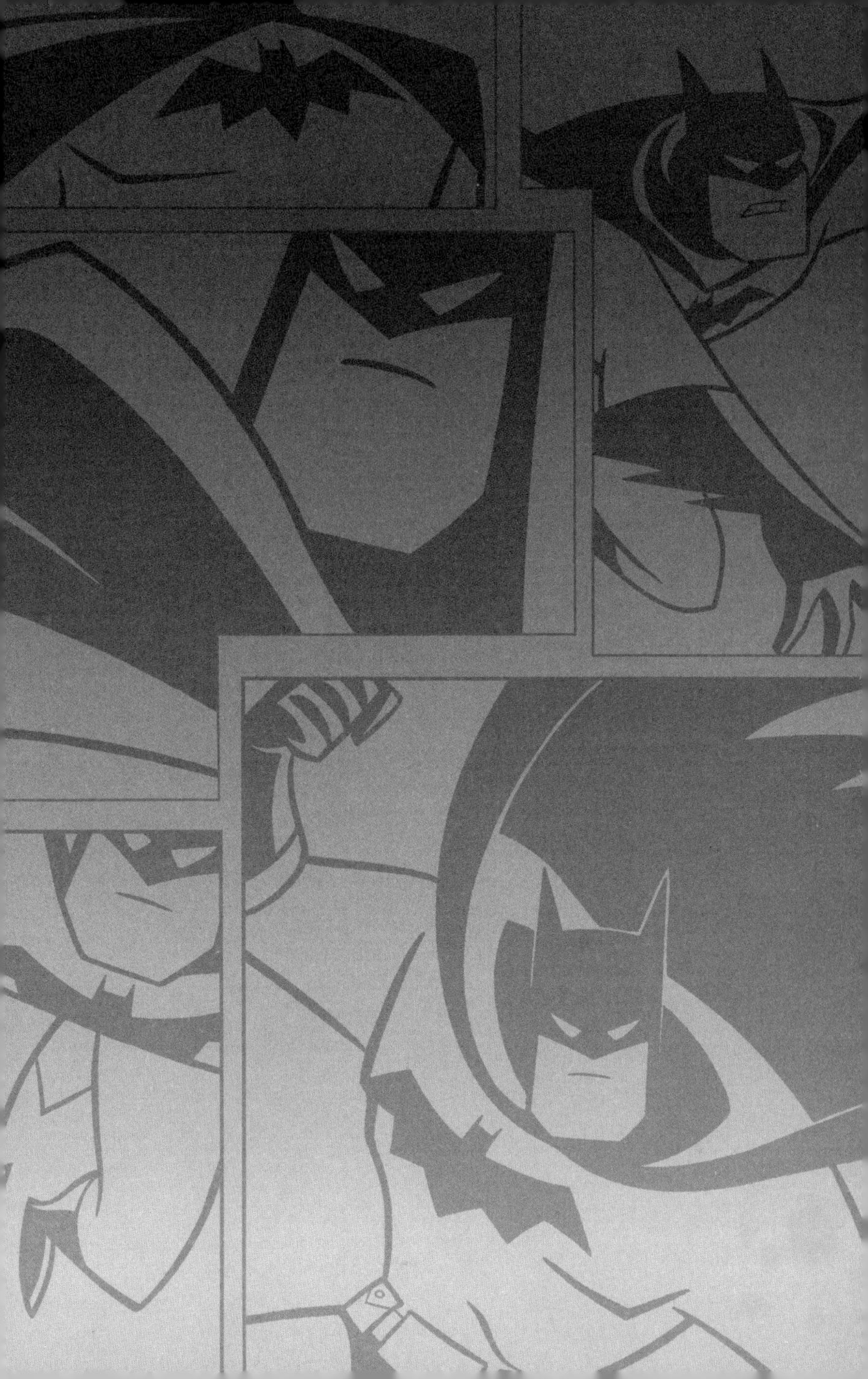

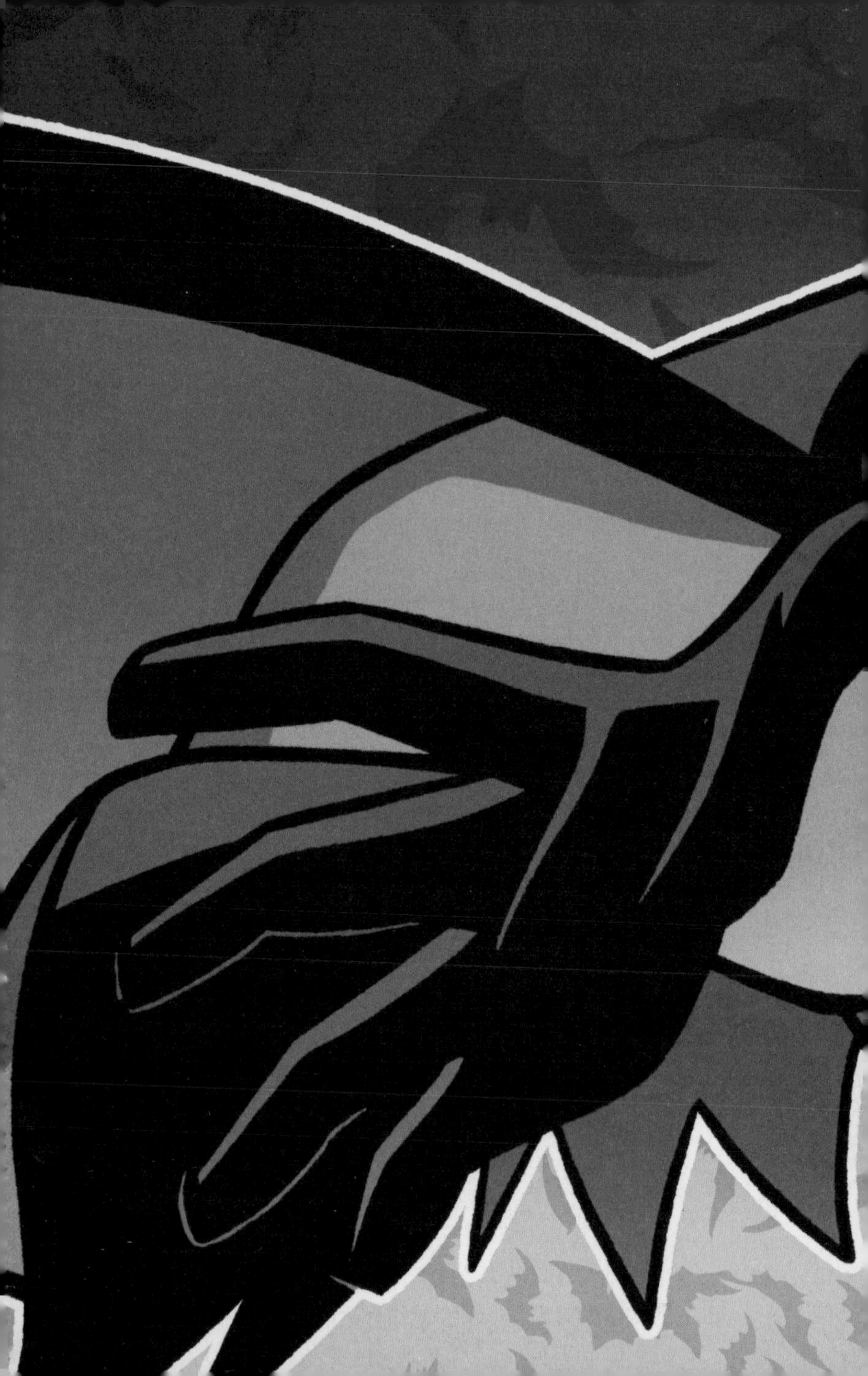